The Purple Kangaroo

Written by

Michael Ian BLACK

AND

Illustrated by

Peter BROWN

simon & schuster books for young readers

new york ✳ london ✳ toronto ✳ sydney

SIMON & SCHUSTER BOOKS FOR YOUNG READERS
An imprint of Simon & Schuster Children's Publishing Division
1230 Avenue of the Americas, New York, New York 10020
Text copyright © 2010 by Hot Schwartz Productions
Illustrations copyright © 2010 by Peter Brown

Book design by Lizzy Bromley
The text for this book is set in Jerky Trash.
The illustrations for this book are
rendered in acrylic paint and graphite with
a wee bit of digital tweaking.
Manufactured in China
2 4 6 8 10 9 7 5 3 1

Library of Congress Cataloging-in-Publication Data
Black, Michael Ian.
The purple kangaroo / Michael Ian Black ; illustrated by Peter Brown.—1st ed.
p. cm. * Summary: After asking the reader to think of something spectacular,
the narrator sets out to prove his ability to read minds by describing
a preposterous situation and characters.
ISBN: 978-1-4169-5771-3 (hardcover : alk. paper)
[1. Imagination—Fiction. 2. Telepathy—Fiction. 3. Humorous stories.]
I. Brown, Peter, 1979– ill. II. Title.
PZ7.B5292Pur 2010 * [E]—dc22 * 2008003534

first
edition

For Evan and Alec,
two terrific nephews
—M. I. B.

For my mom!!!
—P. B.

Hey, kid.

Guess what? I've got a supersecret, highly unusual, incredible, and amazing magical power.

I can read minds.

It's true. In fact, I can read YOUR mind.

I want you to close your eyes and think of something.

What kind of something?

Something spectacular.

I want you to think of something so spectacular that nobody has ever thought of it in the entire history of thinking about things.

MIND READER

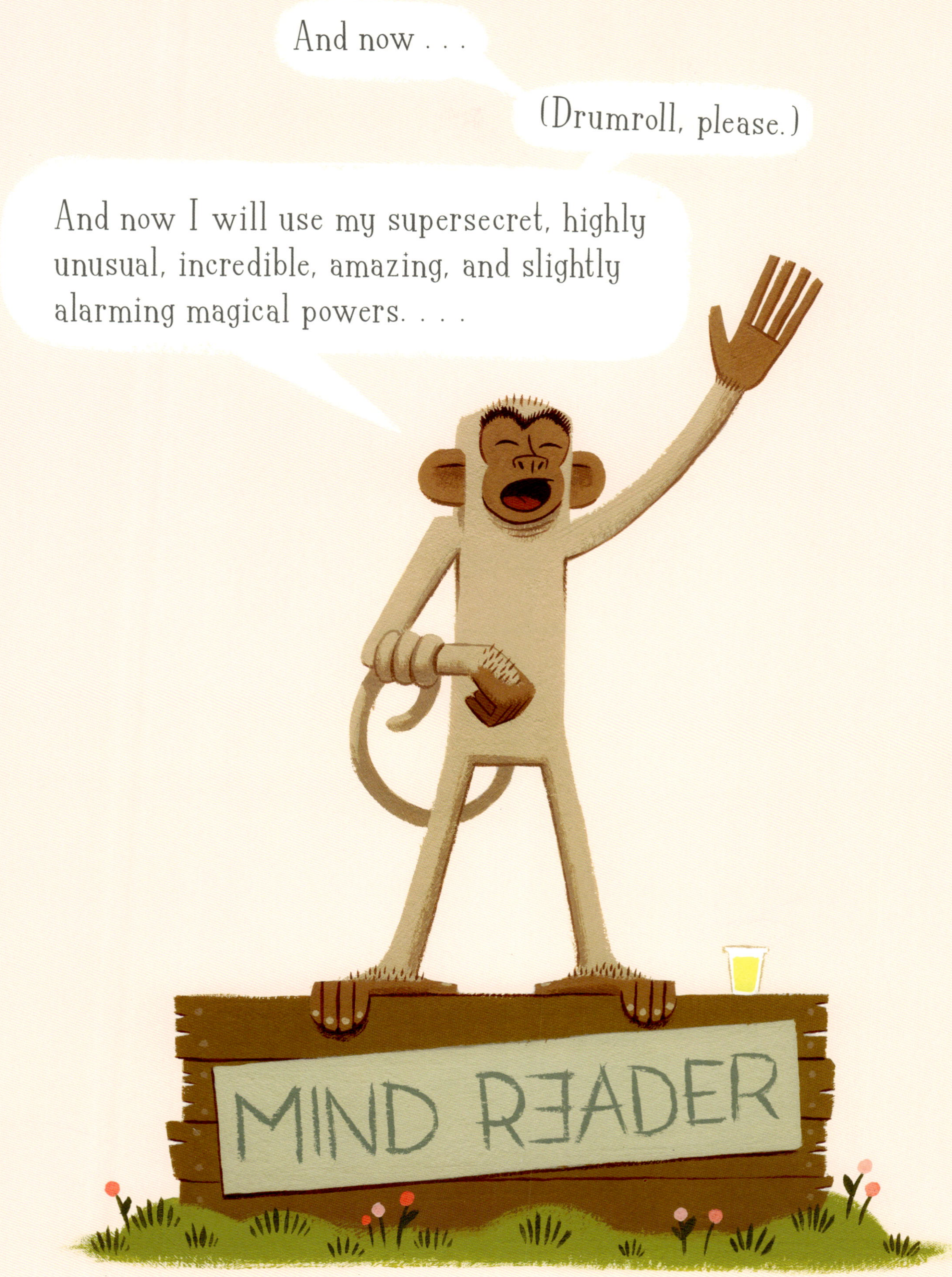
And now . . .
(Drumroll, please.)
And now I will use my supersecret, highly unusual, incredible, amazing, and slightly alarming magical powers. . . .
MIND READER

Look into my eyes. Look deeeeep into my eyes. Concentrate . . . wait! I see something. It's becoming clearer . . . clearer . . .

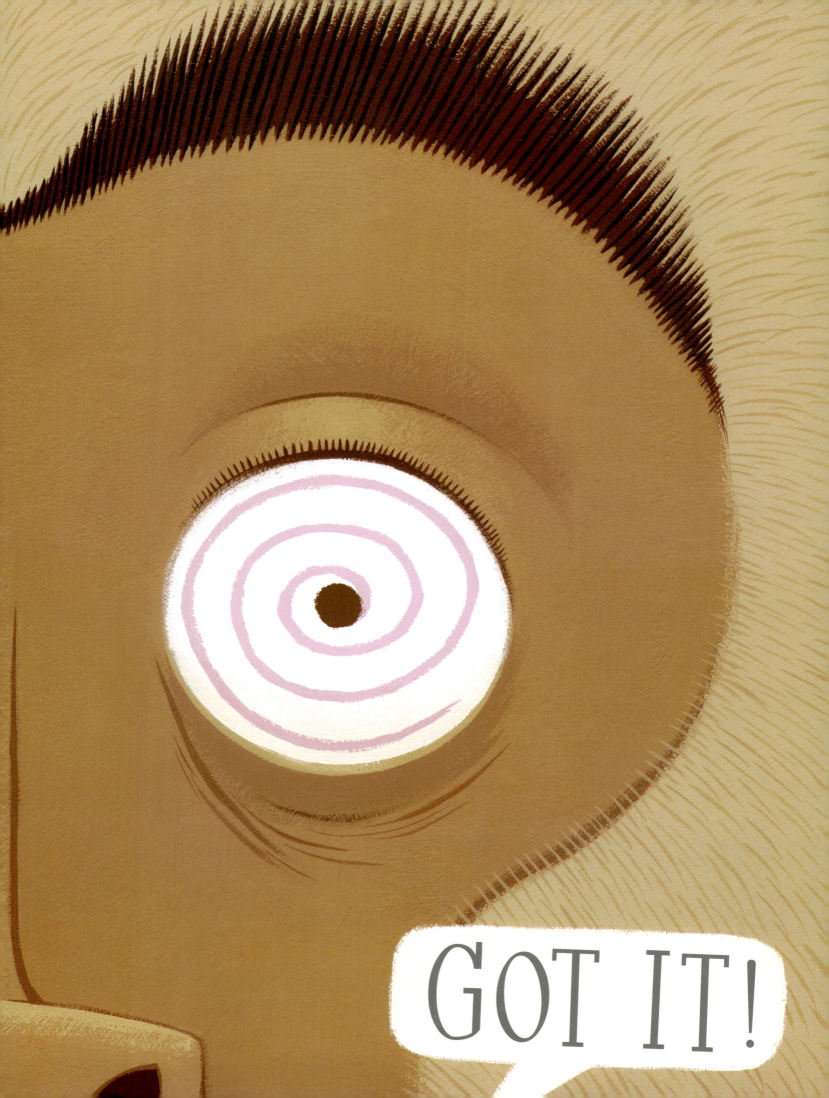

You were thinking about a purple kangaroo!

No?

You weren't thinking about a purple kangaroo?

That's strange.

Do you mean to tell me that you weren't thinking about a purple kangaroo looking for his best friend, a wild-eyed chinchilla named Señor Ernesto de Pantalones?

So, in the course of his search, this purple kangaroo (WHOSE NAME I WOULD LIKE YOU TO NOW PROVIDE) didn't find five fragrant bananas?

While blowing an enormous rainbow bubble-gum bubble out of his nose?

And that a crowd of excited onlookers, upon seeing this astounding trick, didn't shower (INSERT NAME OF PURPLE KANGAROO HERE) with gold coins?

OU SEEN

STO?

Which he then used to hire a giant paisley blimp, thus furthering his search for his very best friend, the wild-eyed chinchilla Señor Ernesto de Pantalones?

And that, while aboard this blimp, he didn't entertain the pilot, Admiral Margarita Flowerpuffer, with feats of hula-hooping derring-do?

HAVE YOU

ERNEST

Are you really going to sit there and tell me that you weren't thinking about a banana-juggling, roller-skating, hula-hooping, rainbow-bubble-gum-nose-blowing, paisley-patterned-blimp-floating, wild-eyed-chinchilla Señor Ernesto de Pantalones-searching purple kangaroo?

On the moon?

Really?

Well, guess what?